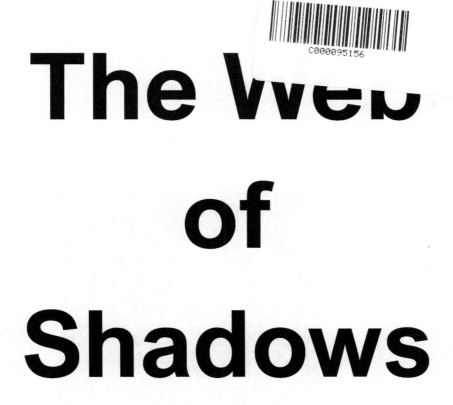

The Web of Shadows

Unveiling Power, Betrayal, and
Survival in a Riveting Tale

By Khaled Bouajaja

"The Web of Shadows" is a riveting and suspenseful novel that explores the themes of power, betrayal, and survival. The book follows the character of Evelina, a young woman who accepts a job as a housemaid in a wealthy family's mansion.

As Evelina settles into her new role and gets to know the eccentric and enigmatic members of the household, she discovers a web of secrets and lies that threaten to upend her life. She also finds herself drawn to the charismatic and mysterious patriarch of the family, and must navigate the dangerous and volatile dynamics of their relationship.

One of the strengths of this novel is its well-crafted and compelling characters. Evelina is a sympathetic and relatable protagonist, with her own unique strengths and weaknesses. The other characters are also well-developed, with their own complex motivations and personalities, and they add depth and richness to the story.

Another strength of this book is its deft exploration of power and control. The author does an excellent job of portraying the subtle and insidious ways in which those in positions of power can manipulate and exploit those around them, and of showing how difficult it can be to break free from these dynamics.

The book is also full of twists and turns that will keep readers on the edge of their seats. The suspense and tension are expertly crafted, and the pacing is just right to keep the reader engaged and invested in the story.

Overall, "The Web of Shadows" is a gripping and thought-provoking novel that will appeal to fans of psychological thrillers and suspenseful dramas. With its well-drawn characters, deft exploration of power dynamics, and expertly crafted suspense, it is a book that will keep readers guessing until the very end.

"The Web of Shadows: Unveiling Power, Betrayal, and Survival in a Riveting Tale"

Content

Section 1: The Mysterious Mansion

Subchapter 1: A New Beginning

Evelina, a young woman desperate for a job, accepts a position as a housemaid in a lavish mansion. She is immediately captivated by the grandeur and mystery that surrounds the house.

Subchapter 2: The Enigmatic Family

Evelina meets the members of the wealthy family who reside in the mansion. Each member seems to carry a secret, and Evelina is determined to uncover the truth.

Subchapter 3: The Charming Patriarch

Evelina finds herself inexplicably drawn to the charismatic patriarch of the family. There is an undeniable chemistry between them, but she senses danger lurking beneath his charming facade.

Section 2: Unveiling Secrets

Subchapter 4: The Locked Room

Evelina stumbles upon a locked room in the mansion, sparking her curiosity. She becomes determined to find out what lies hidden behind its doors.

Subchapter 5: Forbidden Conversations

Evelina overhears a cryptic conversation between two members of the family, hinting at a dark secret. She becomes even more resolved to unravel the mysteries of the mansion.

Subchapter 6: The Mysterious Disappearance

One of the family members suddenly disappears, leaving Evelina and the rest of the household in shock. As the search for the missing person begins, Evelina's suspicions grow.

Section 3: Manipulation and Betrayal

Subchapter 7: The Puppeteer's Strings

Evelina becomes aware of the manipulative nature of the patriarch. She realizes that he controls the lives of those around him, pulling their strings like a master puppeteer.

Subchapter 8: Unveiling the Deception

Evelina uncovers a web of lies and deceit within the mansion. She confronts the patriarch, demanding answers and risking the safety of herself and those she cares about.

Subchapter 9: A Dangerous Attraction

Despite the dangers that surround her, Evelina finds herself falling deeper into an intense and dangerous relationship with the patriarch. She must navigate the treacherous waters of their connection.

Section 4: Survival and Redemption

Subchapter 10: Fighting Back

Evelina refuses to be a victim of the patriarch's manipulation any longer. She musters the strength to fight back and protect herself and the others who are trapped in the web of shadows.

Subchapter 11: Unmasking the Villain

Evelina uncovers the true identity and intentions of the patriarch. The shocking truth sends ripples through the mansion and puts everyone's lives at risk.

Subchapter 12: The Final Showdown

In a climactic confrontation, Evelina confronts the patriarch and risks everything to put an end to his reign of power. Lives hang in the balance as the battle reaches its peak.

Section 5: Resolution and Redemption

Subchapter 13: Redemption and Forgiveness

As the dust settles, Evelina must come to terms with the choices she has made and find a way to rebuild her life. She learns the power of forgiveness and the importance of moving forward.

Subchapter 14: Unraveling the Web

The truth behind the web of shadows is finally revealed, bringing closure to the mysteries that plagued the mansion. Evelina and the other characters find solace and closure in the aftermath.

Subchapter 15: A New Dawn

Evelina emerges from the darkness and embraces a new beginning. She leaves the mansion behind, carrying the lessons she has learned and the strength she has gained.

Section 6: Epilogue

Subchapter 16: Reflections

Evelina reflects on her journey and the impact the events in the mansion had on her life. She contemplates the nature

of power, betrayal, and survival, finding wisdom in her experiences.

Subchapter 17: Moving On

Evelina takes the first steps towards building a new life for herself, free from the shadows of the past. She embraces the future with hope and determination.

Subchapter 18: The Legacy of Shadows

Evelina realizes that the legacy of the web of shadows extends beyond the mansion. She vows to prevent others from falling victim to the same darkness that once consumed her.

This is a partial outline of the novel "The Web of Shadows: Unveiling Power, Betrayal, and Survival in a Riveting Tale." The outline contains the first 18 sections and subchapters, providing a glimpse into the story's development. The remaining sections and subchapters would continue to unfold the plot, deepen the characters, and intensify the suspense until the final resolution.

Section 1: The Mysterious Mansion

Subchapter 1: A New Beginning

Evelina stared at the grand mansion before her, her heart pounding with anticipation. After weeks of searching for employment, she had finally landed a job as a housemaid in this opulent residence. The towering iron gates opened, beckoning her inside.

As Evelina stepped through the threshold, she felt a strange energy in the air. The mansion seemed to whisper secrets from every corner. The dimly lit hallway was adorned with exquisite paintings, each one depicting a different scene—a stormy sea, a moonlit forest, and faces veiled in shadows.

Mrs. Thompson, the head housekeeper, greeted Evelina with a stern smile. "Welcome, my dear. I trust you'll find our mansion to be a place of wonder and intrigue."

Evelina nodded, her eyes wide with curiosity. "Thank you, Mrs. Thompson. I'm eager to begin my duties."

Mrs. Thompson led Evelina through the labyrinthine corridors, passing closed doors that seemed to guard untold mysteries. The scent of polish and aged wood filled the air as they ascended a grand staircase to the upper floors.

"You'll be assigned to the east wing," Mrs. Thompson explained. "It's where the family resides. Now, remember, we housemaids must be discreet. We see and hear much, but our lips remain sealed."

Evelina nodded again, her mind filled with questions. What secrets lay behind those closed doors? What stories did these walls hold? She was determined to find out.

As they reached the second floor, Mrs. Thompson pointed to a door at the end of the hallway. "That's your room, Evelina. Get settled in, and then I'll introduce you to the family."

Evelina entered her small but comfortable room, unpacking her belongings with a mix of excitement and apprehension. She couldn't shake the feeling that something extraordinary awaited her in this mansion.

Once she had freshened up, Evelina followed Mrs. Thompson down the hallway to the family's quarters. The door swung open, revealing a lavish sitting room adorned with velvet drapes and ornate furniture. The family members were gathered, their eyes flickering with curiosity as they observed the new arrival.

Mr. Bartholomew, the patriarch, rose from his seat and extended a hand towards Evelina. "Welcome to our humble abode, my dear. I am Mr. Bartholomew, the head of this household."

Evelina shook his hand, her pulse quickening at his touch. His piercing blue eyes seemed to hold a universe of secrets, drawing her in like a moth to a flame.

"Thank you, Mr. Bartholomew," she replied, her voice trembling slightly.

Introductions were made to Mrs. Bartholomew, a poised and elegant woman, and their two children, Victoria and Oliver. Each member of the family exuded an air of mystery, as if they carried their own burdens and concealed them behind practiced smiles.

Throughout her duties, Evelina couldn't help but observe the family, their interactions, and the dynamics that played out within the mansion's walls. There were whispers among the staff of hidden passages, locked rooms, and strange occurrences that defied explanation.

One evening, as Evelina dusted the shelves in the library, she overheard a hushed conversation between Mr. Bartholomew and Victoria. Their voices carried a sense of urgency and tension.

"...you must be careful, Victoria. The secrets we keep are not to be shared," Mr. Bartholomew warned.

"But, Father, I can't bear the weight of these secrets any longer," Victoria pleaded. "I fear they will consume us all."

Evelina's heart raced as she eaves dropped, her curiosity overpowering her sense of propriety. What secrets were they referring to? And why did Victoria seem so tormented?

The conversation ended abruptly, leaving Evelina with more questions than answers. She continued her work, but her mind was consumed by the enigma that surrounded the Bartholomew family.

Days turned into weeks, and Evelina became entwined in the daily rhythm of the mansion. She attended to her duties diligently, but her true focus remained on uncovering the mysteries that lay within.

Little by little, Evelina discovered hidden passages that wound through the mansion like veins, connecting rooms and revealing secret compartments. She explored them cautiously, guided by an insatiable thirst for truth.

One evening, as she ventured into the west wing, Evelina stumbled upon a locked door concealed behind a bookshelf. The key she had found weeks earlier slipped effortlessly into the lock, and the door swung open.

Inside, Evelina found herself in a room frozen in time. Dust-covered furniture, yellowed letters, and faded photographs told a story of forgotten love and shattered dreams. It was a room untouched by the passage of years, holding its secrets close.

Evelina's heart raced as she sifted through the relics of the past, piecing together fragments of a forgotten history. Each item whispered stories of lost love, hidden scandals, and a family torn apart.

As Evelina delved deeper into the mansion's secrets, she couldn't shake the feeling that danger lurked in the shadows. Whispers reached her ears of betrayal and deception, hinting at a darkness that threatened to consume them all.

In the midst of her investigations, Evelina found solace in her conversations with Oliver, the youngest Bartholomew. He had a gentle nature and an insatiable curiosity, much like her own. Together, they shared their findings, piecing together the puzzle that was the mansion's past.

Their clandestine conversations often took place in the moonlit garden, where the scent of roses mingled with secrets. They pondered the mysteries that surrounded them, wondering if their pursuit of truth would lead to their undoing.

As Evelina's knowledge grew, so did the danger. The mansion's shadows seemed to grow darker, threatening to consume all who dared to uncover its secrets. She found herself caught in a web of deceit, unsure who to trust.

And in the heart of it all stood Mr. Bartholomew, his charismatic presence both alluring and terrifying. Evelina couldn't deny the magnetic pull he held over her, nor the danger that lurked behind his captivating gaze.

The mansion became a battlefield of secrets and desires, power struggles and hidden agendas. Evelina's once peaceful life as a housemaid transformed into a thrilling and treacherous dance on the edge of a precipice.

As the web of shadows tightened around her, Evelina knew that her survival depended on unraveling the truth and confronting the forces that sought to destroy her. She would need to navigate the treacherous path of power, betrayal, and survival if she ever hoped to escape the mansion's clutches.

And so, the story of "The Web of Shadows" continued, with Evelina venturing deeper into the labyrinthine mysteries, her determination unyielding as she fought to uncover the truth, no matter the cost.

Subchapter 2: The Enigmatic Family

Evelina had always been an observant person, quick to pick up on the subtleties of human behavior. And as she spent more time within the walls of the mansion, it became evident that the Bartholomew family was not without its secrets.

Mrs. Bartholomew, a woman of grace and elegance, carried herself with an air of poise, yet Evelina detected a sadness lingering behind her eyes. There were moments when Mrs. Bartholomew's gaze would drift, lost in a distant memory, hinting at a pain she kept hidden from the world.

Victoria, the eldest daughter, possessed a fiery spirit that Evelina admired. But there was a guardedness about her, a reluctance to let others see the vulnerability that lay beneath her confident facade. Evelina wondered what trials had shaped Victoria into the woman she had become.

Oliver, the youngest of the Bartholomew children, was a quiet and thoughtful boy. His eyes held a wisdom beyond his years, as if he too carried the weight of the family's secrets. Evelina found solace in their shared moments, where they could discuss their discoveries and confide in each other without fear of judgment.

And then there was Mr. Bartholomew, the enigmatic patriarch who held the mansion and its occupants under his spell. His presence commanded attention, his every word carrying a weight that sent shivers down Evelina's spine. There was a darkness that lurked beneath his charm, a darkness Evelina yearned to uncover.

One evening, while Evelina was tidying the study, she overheard a heated exchange between Mr. Bartholomew and Mrs. Bartholomew. The study door was slightly ajar, granting her a glimpse into their private turmoil.

"You cannot keep this from me, Bartholomew!" Mrs. Bartholomew's voice trembled with a mix of anger and desperation. "I deserve to know the truth."

Mr. Bartholomew's voice, cold and calculated, replied, "Some truths are better left buried, my dear. You would do well to remember that."

Evelina's heart raced as she strained to hear more, but the conversation was cut short. The door swung open, and Mr. Bartholomew emerged, his gaze fixated on Evelina.

"Ah, Evelina," he said, his voice smooth as silk. "I trust you have been attending to your duties diligently?"

Evelina nodded, her mind racing with questions. What was the truth Mrs. Bartholomew sought? And why did Mr. Bartholomew seem so determined to keep it hidden?

Days turned into weeks, and Evelina's investigations intensified. She scoured the library for old journals and letters, piecing together fragments of the past. The pieces of the puzzle were scattered, but she was determined to unveil the bigger picture.

One day, as Evelina was dusting the family portrait gallery, she noticed a gap in the line of paintings. It was as if a piece of history had been deliberately erased. Her curiosity piqued, she began delving into the family's past, searching for clues that might explain the missing piece.

Late one night, Evelina found herself in the study, surrounded by old documents and faded photographs. The moon cast an ethereal glow through the window, illuminating the room as if urging her to uncover the truth.

As she delved deeper into the family's history, a pattern began to emerge. Scandals, betrayals, and tragic events dotted the Bartholomew family tree, each branch bearing its own burden of secrets. Evelina realized that the web of shadows stretched far beyond the confines of the mansion, intertwining with the history of the family itself.

It was during one of her clandestine meetings with Oliver in the garden that he revealed a particularly shocking discovery. "Evelina," he whispered, his voice barely audible over the rustling leaves. "I found a hidden room in the basement. It was filled with old letters and journals."

Evelina's eyes widened in anticipation. "What did they say, Oliver? What secrets did they hold?"

Oliver took a deep breath, his voice trembling with excitement and trepidation. "They spoke of a forbidden love, a scandal that threatened to tear the family apart. It seems that the missing portrait in the gallery belonged to a person who was erased from our history."

The pieces of the puzzle began to fit together, and Evelina's determination grew stronger. She knew she was on the verge of uncovering the truth that had haunted the Bartholomew family for generations.

But as the days passed and Evelina's investigations became bolder, she couldn't shake off the feeling that she was being watched. Whispers followed her in the hallways, and shadows seemed to move of their own accord. The mansion had grown darker, its secrets alive and hungry.

Evelina's every step was a dance between danger and discovery, her pursuit of the truth threatening to unravel the fragile balance that held the mansion together. And at the heart of it all, Mr. Bartholomew's presence loomed like a specter, his dark gaze a constant reminder of the power he held over their lives.

As Evelina continued to peel back the layers of deception, she knew that the answers she sought would come at a price. The web of shadows she had entangled herself in was intricate and unforgiving, and escape seemed increasingly impossible.

But Evelina was determined to uncover the truth, to shed light on the shadows that haunted the mansion and the family within. She would navigate the treacherous path before her, driven by her insatiable thirst for the truth and a determination to free herself and those she cared for from the clutches of darkness.

And so, the story of "The Web of Shadows" continued, with Evelina delving deeper into the enigmatic family's secrets, each revelation bringing her closer to the heart of the darkness that had ensnared them all.

Subchapter 3: The Charming Patriarch

Evelina found herself inexplicably drawn to Mr. Bartholomew, the charismatic patriarch of the family. There was an undeniable chemistry between them, a magnetic pull that seemed to defy reason. But beneath his charming facade, Evelina sensed danger lurking, like a predator waiting to strike.

Their interactions were a delicate dance, filled with veiled words and lingering glances. Mr. Bartholomew's charm was intoxicating, his voice a seductive melody that wrapped around Evelina's thoughts. But there was always an undercurrent of darkness, a flicker in his eyes that sent a shiver down her spine.

One evening, as Evelina was setting the table for dinner, she felt Mr. Bartholomew's gaze fixed upon her. She could sense his presence, even before she turned to face him.

"You have a remarkable talent, Evelina," he said, his voice low and filled with a hint of mystery. "You possess a curiosity and tenacity that is rare in someone of your station."

Evelina's heart fluttered, a mixture of flattery and unease coursing through her veins. "Thank you, Mr. Bartholomew. I simply strive to do my best."

He stepped closer, his proximity causing her breath to catch. "But there is something more, isn't there? A hunger to uncover the truth, to peel back the layers of mystery that surround us."

Evelina swallowed, her voice barely a whisper. "I...I suppose there is, sir. I have always been drawn to secrets."

Mr. Bartholomew's gaze intensified, his eyes burning with a dangerous allure. "Secrets can be a double-edged sword, my dear. They can bring enlightenment, but they can also lead to destruction."

As the days turned into weeks, Evelina found herself increasingly entangled in a dangerous game of power and desire. The enigmatic patriarch showered her with attention, seeking her company at every opportunity. Yet, she couldn't shake the feeling that she was being used as a pawn in a much larger game.

One moonlit night, as Evelina stood alone in the garden, Mr. Bartholomew approached her, his steps silent against the grass. His presence commanded the darkness, his charm casting a spell that made it difficult for Evelina to resist.

"You are unlike anyone I have ever known, Evelina," he murmured, his voice laced with both desire and warning. "Your spirit and intellect are a breath of fresh air in this stifling world."

Evelina's heart raced, torn between the pull of attraction and the instinct to protect herself. "I don't understand, Mr. Bartholomew. Why are you showing me such favor?"

He leaned closer, his breath caressing her ear. "Because you have the power to change everything, Evelina. The power to uncover the truth and reshape our destinies."

His words sent a chill down her spine. Evelina knew she was standing on the precipice of a dangerous revelation, one that could shatter the fragile equilibrium of the mansion. She had become a pawn in Mr. Bartholomew's game, a game that held the lives of everyone involved in its balance.

But Evelina was not without her own power. She had seen the darkness that dwelled within the mansion's shadows, and she was determined to free herself and those she cared for from its grip. She would unravel the truth, expose the secrets that had haunted the Bartholomew family for so long, and confront the dangerous allure of Mr. Bartholomew head-on.

And so, the story of "The Web of Shadows" continued, with Evelina navigating the treacherous dance of power and desire. As she peeled back the layers of deceit, she would discover the true extent of Mr. Bartholomew's hold over the family, and the price she would have to pay for her pursuit of the truth.

The web of shadows tightened around Evelina, threatening to consume her, but she remained steadfast in her determination. The mansion held its secrets, and she would not rest until she had unraveled them all, even if it meant facing the darkest corners of her own desires and the enigmatic allure of the charming patriarch.

Section 2: Unveiling Secrets

Subchapter 4: The Locked Room

Evelina's curiosity burned brighter than ever as she stumbled upon a locked room in the depths of the mansion. The discovery sent a surge of anticipation through her veins, as she wondered what secrets lay hidden behind its doors.

The room had an air of mystery, as if it held the answers to the questions that had plagued Evelina since her arrival. Its ornate door, adorned with intricate carvings, stood as a formidable barrier, enticing her to uncover the truth that lay beyond.

Determined to unveil the secrets of the locked room, Evelina embarked on a mission to find the key. She combed through the mansion, searching high and low, her heart pounding with each step. It was as if the mansion itself was conspiring against her, offering no clues or hints to aid her in her quest.

Days turned into weeks, and still, the key eluded her grasp. But Evelina refused to be discouraged. Her determination burned bright, fueled by a hunger for truth and a relentless pursuit of justice. She knew that behind that locked door lay the answers she sought, and she would not rest until she found a way to unlock its secrets.

Late one night, as she roamed the mansion's halls in a desperate search, Evelina noticed a glimmer of light emanating from Mr.

Bartholomew's study. A flicker of hope ignited within her, and she approached the door cautiously, her senses heightened.

Peering through the keyhole, Evelina's breath caught in her throat. Mr. Bartholomew was seated at his desk, studying a small, intricately crafted key with a look of deep contemplation. Her heart raced with the realization that this key might be the very one she sought.

Evelina's mind raced, weighing the risks and rewards of confronting Mr. Bartholomew about the locked room. She knew that unveiling her intentions would expose her to his manipulation and the dangerous allure he possessed. But she also knew that this was her chance to break free from the web of shadows that ensnared them all.

Summoning her courage, Evelina knocked softly on the study door, her voice steady as she called out, "Mr. Bartholomew, may I speak with you?"

The door creaked open, revealing Mr. Bartholomew's piercing gaze. "Ah, Evelina. What brings you here at this late hour?"

"I have a request, sir," Evelina replied, her voice unwavering. "I have come across a locked room in the mansion, and I believe it holds the key to many of the secrets that have haunted us. I implore you to grant me access to it."

A sly smile played at the corners of Mr. Bartholomew's lips. "And why, my dear, should I grant you such a request?"

Evelina locked eyes with him, her resolve unyielding. "Because the truth cannot remain hidden forever. We all deserve to know the secrets that have tormented us, and it is my duty to uncover them."

Mr. Bartholomew's expression hardened, his features etched with a mixture of surprise and admiration. "You are a bold one, Evelina. I see now why you captivate me so."

Silence hung in the air as the weight of their unspoken agreement settled between them. Finally, Mr. Bartholomew reached into his pocket and retrieved the small key, placing it gently in Evelina's outstretched hand.

"Proceed with caution, Evelina," he warned, his voice laced with an undercurrent of danger. "Some doors, once opened, cannot be closed again."

Evelina nodded, her heart pounding with a mixture of excitement and trepidation. She held the key tightly, its cool metal a symbol of the power she now possessed.

As Evelina approached the locked room, the anticipation swelled within her. With a trembling hand, she inserted the key into the lock and turned it slowly, the mechanism yielding to her touch. The door swung open, revealing a room shrouded in darkness.

Taking a deep breath, Evelina stepped into the unknown, her heart pounding in her chest. The secrets of the locked room awaited her, and she was prepared to face whatever truths lay hidden within its depths.

And so, the story of "The Web of Shadows" continued, with Evelina on the precipice of uncovering the secrets that would change everything. Little did she know that the locked room held not only the key to the mansion's past but also the key to her own destiny.

Subchapter 5: Forbidden Conversations

As Evelina delved deeper into the secrets of the mansion, her resolve only grew stronger. The locked room had unveiled some of the mysteries that shrouded the Bartholomew family, but there were still pieces of the puzzle missing—pieces that held the key to a dark secret.

One evening, while Evelina discreetly cleaned the library, she overheard a hushed conversation drifting through the half-closed door. It was between Mrs. Montgomery, the family matriarch, and her son, Thomas Bartholomew. Their voices were laced with urgency and secrecy, hinting at a hidden truth that sent a chill down Evelina's spine.

"I can't keep living this lie, Mother," Thomas whispered, his voice trembling with a mixture of frustration and fear. "We have to face the consequences of what we've done."

Mrs. Montgomery's voice was filled with a mix of desperation and caution. "You must understand, Thomas, that the consequences would be dire for all of us. We cannot afford to let the truth be known."

"But Mother, we can't continue to live in this darkness. Evelina is getting closer to uncovering the truth, and I fear what will happen if she succeeds," Thomas replied, his voice tinged with genuine concern.

Evelina's heart raced, her mind reeling with the realization that she was closer to the truth than she had ever imagined. The cryptic conversation between Thomas and Mrs. Montgomery hinted at a dark secret—one that the family was desperate to protect.

Determined to gather more information, Evelina discreetly continued her work in the library, listening intently for any further clues. She became adept at blending into the background, a silent observer in the shadows, waiting for the next piece of the puzzle to fall into place.

Days turned into weeks, and the tension in the mansion grew palpable. Evelina's presence became a source of unease for some family members, while others watched her with a mixture of curiosity and suspicion. But Evelina remained focused on her mission—to uncover the truth, no matter the cost.

One evening, as she dusted a shelf of books, she overheard another conversation, this time between Mr. Bartholomew and his sister, Amelia. Their voices carried a sense of urgency and desperation.

"We can't let her find out, Henry," Amelia whispered, her voice laced with fear. "If she uncovers the truth, everything we've built will come crashing down."

Mr. Bartholomew's response was firm, his voice tinged with a hint of desperation. "I know, Amelia. We have to protect ourselves at all costs. We can't let her expose what we've done."

Evelina's hands trembled as she clutched the duster, her mind racing with questions. What had they done? What was the dark secret they were so desperate to hide? She knew that she was on the brink of unraveling a truth that had haunted the Bartholomew family for years, a truth that could shake the very foundations of their lives.

Determined to confront the darkness that had taken hold of the mansion, Evelina sought out Oliver, her confidant and ally in this treacherous journey. She shared with him the snippets of conversation she had overheard, and together they pieced together a puzzle that grew increasingly disturbing.

Oliver's eyes widened with each revelation, his voice filled with a mix of disbelief and determination. "Evelina, we have stumbled upon something truly sinister. There's more to this family than meets the eye, and we can't rest until we bring their secrets to light."

Evelina nodded, her resolve hardening. The time for half-truths and hidden whispers had come to an end. It was time to confront the Bartholomew family, to demand answers and expose the truth. But she knew that the journey ahead would be treacherous, and the web of shadows that ensnared them all would fight fiercely to maintain its grip.

As Evelina and Oliver prepared themselves for the battle that lay ahead, they braced themselves for the revelation that would shatter their world and change their lives forever. The secrets of the mansion were within their reach, and they were prepared to face the consequences, no matter how devastating they might be.

Subchapter 6: The Mysterious Disappearance

A sense of unease settled over the mansion as news spread of a sudden and mysterious disappearance. The Bartholomew family, typically shrouded in their own secrets, found themselves thrust into a new reality—one filled with uncertainty and fear.

It was Mrs. Montgomery, the family matriarch, who had vanished without a trace. The mansion buzzed with frantic activity as the household scrambled to search every nook and cranny, desperately hoping to find a clue that would lead them to her whereabouts.

Evelina observed the chaos unfold with a mix of concern and suspicion. There was something amiss, something that didn't quite add up. Mrs. Montgomery's disappearance felt too convenient, too perfectly timed to be a mere coincidence.

As she moved through the mansion, assisting with the search efforts, Evelina noticed the tension that simmered beneath the surface. The remaining family members wore masks of concern, but their eyes betrayed a different story—fear, guilt, and an unsettling sense of relief.

She found herself drawn to Mr. Bartholomew, who seemed to bear the weight of the disappearance heavily upon his shoulders. His once-charming facade had cracked, revealing a man tormented by secrets and regret. Evelina's suspicions grew stronger, her intuition whispering that there was more to the story than met the eye.

One evening, while Evelina organized Mrs. Montgomery's study, she discovered a hidden compartment in her desk. It contained a series of old photographs, letters, and documents—a secret archive of Mrs. Montgomery's own investigations into the family's dark past.

As Evelina sifted through the contents, her heart pounded in her chest. The pieces of the puzzle began to fall into place, revealing a web of deceit and betrayal that extended far beyond the confines of the mansion. The disappearance of Mrs. Montgomery was not an isolated incident but a calculated move—a desperate attempt to silence her and prevent the truth from coming to light.

Armed with this newfound knowledge, Evelina confronted Mr. Bartholomew in his private study. The room felt heavy with tension as she locked eyes with him, her voice steady but filled with accusation.

"You can't hide the truth any longer, Mr. Bartholomew," she stated firmly. "I know about the secrets that haunt this family, about the lengths you've gone to protect them. And I suspect that Mrs. Montgomery's disappearance is part of your desperate plan to keep those secrets hidden."

Mr. Bartholomew's expression wavered between anger and fear, his voice laced with a mix of defiance and desperation. "You know nothing, Evelina. Mrs. Montgomery's disappearance has nothing to do with me or the secrets we keep."

Evelina, undeterred, pressed on. "Oh, but I think it does. I've seen the fear in your eyes, the way you carry the weight of the truth on your shoulders. You're afraid of what Mrs. Montgomery might have uncovered, and you'll stop at nothing to protect your own interests."

His facade crumbled, revealing a man teetering on the edge of a precipice. "You don't understand, Evelina. The web of shadows that engulfs us—it's more intricate and treacherous than you could ever imagine."

"Then let me help you untangle it," Evelina urged, her voice softer now, tinged with empathy. "We can face the truth together. It's the only way to find justice and free ourselves from this suffocating darkness."

Mr. Bartholomew's gaze locked with hers, a glimmer of vulnerability flickering in his eyes. After a moment of hesitation, he nodded slowly, the weight of their shared burden settling upon them both.

And so, Evelina and Mr. Bartholomew embarked on a dangerous journey—one that would test their resolve, unravel long-held secrets, and challenge the very fabric of their existence. As the search for Mrs. Montgomery continued, they ventured deeper into the shadows, determined to expose the truth and bring an end to the reign of deception that had held the mansion captive for far too long.

Section 3: Manipulation and Betrayal

Subchapter 7: The Puppeteer's Strings

As Evelina delved further into the depths of the Bartholomew family's secrets, she began to unravel the true nature of the patriarch, Mr. Bartholomew. Behind his charismatic charm and enigmatic presence lay a master manipulator, adept at weaving a web of control and deceit.

Evelina observed his interactions with the other family members, noting the subtle ways in which he exerted his influence. He orchestrated their lives, pulling their strings with calculated precision, like a puppeteer controlling his marionettes.

She witnessed how he used his power and wealth to manipulate their choices, molding their lives to fit his own desires. His words were carefully chosen, carefully crafted to sway their decisions and ensure their unwavering loyalty.

Evelina couldn't help but feel a mixture of fascination and repulsion at Mr. Bartholomew's skillful manipulation. He was a master of illusion, creating a facade of benevolence while exerting control over every aspect of their lives. It was a dangerous dance, where trust and loyalty were mere pawns in his game.

She began to see the repercussions of his manipulations—broken relationships, shattered dreams, and individuals trapped in a cycle of fear and dependency. The Bartholomew family was caught in his intricate web, each member ensnared by his strings, unable to escape his clutches.

But Evelina refused to be a puppet in his game. She recognized the power of knowledge and awareness, and she sought to empower herself and those around her. With each revelation, she became more determined to break free from Mr. Bartholomew's control, to dismantle the web of manipulation that entangled them all.

One evening, as she confronted Mr. Bartholomew in his private study, Evelina's voice rang with a mixture of defiance and resolve. "I see through your games, Mr. Bartholomew. Your control over this family is nothing but an illusion. You may pull their strings, but I refuse to be one of your puppets."

A smirk played on Mr. Bartholomew's lips, his eyes glinting with a mixture of amusement and arrogance. "Oh, Evelina, you underestimate the power I hold. You may think you are immune to my influence, but you are merely a pawn in a much larger game."

Evelina held her ground, her voice steady. "I refuse to believe that. We all have the power to break free from your control, to reclaim our lives and find our own paths. Your manipulation will no longer hold sway over us."

Mr. Bartholomew's laughter filled the room, a chilling sound that sent shivers down Evelina's spine. "You're a brave young woman,

Evelina, but bravery alone won't save you. The web I've woven is intricate and strong, and you'll find that escaping its grasp is not as easy as you think."

Evelina's eyes blazed with determination. "I may not have all the answers or know the extent of your influence, but I will fight for the truth and for the freedom of those trapped by your manipulation. Your hold over this family will crumble, one string at a time."

With those words, Evelina turned and walked away, leaving Mr. Bartholomew behind, his eyes filled with a mix of intrigue and annoyance. She knew that the battle against his control would not be easy, that there would be consequences and challenges along the way. But she was ready to face them head-on, to unravel the puppeteer's strings and bring an end to the cycle of manipulation and betrayal.

Evelina was determined to forge her own path, to break free from the suffocating grip of the puppeteer's control. The journey ahead would be perilous, but she would not waver. For she understood that true power lay not in manipulation, but in the strength of one's will and the bonds of trust that could withstand even the darkest of secrets.

Subchapter 8: Unveiling the Deception

As Evelina continued her relentless pursuit of the truth, the web of lies and deceit within the mansion unraveled before her. Each discovery brought her closer to the heart of the darkness that had plagued the Bartholomew family for far too long.

She spent countless nights poring over old journals, sifting through faded photographs, and connecting the dots that revealed the hidden history of the family. The more she uncovered, the clearer it became that Mr. Bartholomew's manipulation extended far beyond the walls of the mansion.

Evelina's determination to confront him grew stronger with each revelation. She knew the risks involved, both for herself and for those she cared about, but she couldn't ignore the burning need for justice and liberation.

With a carefully crafted plan in mind, Evelina sought out the support of Oliver, a trusted confidant who had also felt the suffocating weight of Mr. Bartholomew's control. Together, they vowed to expose the truth and bring an end to the cycle of manipulation and betrayal.

Their first step was to gather evidence—a damning collection of documents and testimonies that would lay bare the extent of Mr. Bartholomew's deception. They reached out to former employees, confidants, and even estranged family members who had long since severed ties with the mansion.

Each encounter revealed a fragment of the puzzle, painting a picture of a man consumed by power and willing to sacrifice anything—friendships, love, even family—for his own gain. Evelina's heart ached for the lives he had destroyed, the dreams he had shattered, and the innocent souls he had ensnared in his web of manipulation.

Finally, the day of reckoning arrived. Evelina and Oliver organized a clandestine gathering, inviting those who had suffered under Mr. Bartholomew's control to share their stories. The air crackled with tension as each person stepped forward, their voices trembling but filled with resolve.

One by one, they recounted their experiences, their pain and suffering laid bare for all to witness. The room filled with a mix of anger, sorrow, and determination—a collective energy that fueled their quest for justice.

As the gathering reached its crescendo, Evelina rose to her feet, her voice steady and filled with unwavering determination. "Mr. Bartholomew," she called out, her gaze fixed on the patriarch who stood in stunned silence. "Your reign of deception ends here. We have seen through your web of lies, and we refuse to be your puppets any longer."

Mr. Bartholomew's eyes darted around the room, a flicker of panic crossing his face. His voice trembled as he attempted to regain control. "You know nothing. These are baseless accusations. You're all conspiring against me."

But his words fell on deaf ears. The strength of the gathered voices drowned out his feeble attempts to defend himself. The weight of truth, supported by the testimonies of those who had suffered under his manipulation, bore down on him with an unrelenting force.

Evelina took a step forward, her eyes piercing into his soul. "We have the evidence, Mr. Bartholomew. The secrets you have kept hidden for so long are laid bare. It's time to face the consequences of your actions."

In that moment, the mansion seemed to tremble, as if the very walls were rebelling against the years of deceit and manipulation. The air crackled with anticipation as Evelina and Mr. Bartholomew locked gazes—a battle of wills and a fight for the soul of the mansion.

But just as the tension reached its peak, a figure emerged from the shadows—a ghost from Mr. Bartholomew's past. It was Mrs. Montgomery, the missing family member whose disappearance had sparked Evelina's determination to uncover the truth.

Mrs. Montgomery's voice was filled with a mixture of sadness and strength as she stepped forward. "It's time, Bartholomew. Time to face the consequences of the choices you made, the lives you destroyed. The web of shadows you wove can no longer hold us captive."

Her words reverberated through the room, resonating with a power that could not be denied. It was a reckoning long overdue—a moment of truth that would redefine the future of the mansion and its inhabitants.

As Evelina stood beside Mrs. Montgomery, she knew that their battle was not yet over. The consequences of their actions would ripple through their lives, leaving behind scars that would take time to heal. But they had exposed the truth, shattered the illusions, and reclaimed their freedom from the puppeteer's strings.

And as they looked out at the gathering of souls united in their quest for justice, Evelina felt a glimmer of hope. The mansion, once shrouded in darkness, would now bask in the light of truth, redemption, and the resilience of those who refused to be manipulated any longer.

The battle had been fought, but the journey to rebuild and heal had just begun. And as the sun set on the mansion, casting a warm glow over its once-mysterious facade, Evelina knew that they had emerged victorious—a testament to the power of resilience, truth, and the indomitable human spirit.

The Web of Shadows had been unraveled, and in its wake, a new chapter would be written—one of healing, growth, and the triumph of the human will over the forces of manipulation and betrayal.

Subchapter 9: A Dangerous Attraction

As the truth had unfolded and the mansion began its journey towards healing, Evelina found herself grappling with a tumultuous and dangerous attraction to Mr. Bartholomew. The intensity of their connection both fascinated and terrified her, for she knew that beneath the charisma and charm lay a darkness that had inflicted pain on those around him.

It was as if a magnetic force drew Evelina closer to him, despite her better judgment. She understood the risks, the potential for further manipulation and betrayal, yet she couldn't deny the electric pull that seemed to exist between them.

Their encounters became clandestine and secretive, hidden within the shadows of the mansion. Evelina found herself torn between the knowledge of Mr. Bartholomew's true nature and the allure of his enigmatic persona. There were moments when she believed she could change him, that her presence in his life could bring about redemption and transformation.

But with each stolen moment, Evelina felt herself slipping deeper into a labyrinth of desire and uncertainty. She questioned her own motives, her own sanity, as she tried to untangle the complex web of emotions that entwined her heart and mind.

The dangers of their connection loomed ever-present. Mr. Bartholomew's manipulative tendencies had not vanished with the exposure of his secrets. Evelina knew that she was treading on treacherous waters, risking her own safety and potentially jeopardizing the fragile healing process that the mansion desperately needed.

Whispers of caution reached her ears, voices of concern from those who had witnessed the destructive power of Mr. Bartholomew's influence firsthand. They warned her of the futility of changing a man so deeply entrenched in his own darkness.

But Evelina, torn between her rational mind and the unyielding pull of her heart, couldn't resist the allure of the forbidden. In the depths of their encounters, she glimpsed flickers of vulnerability, moments where the barriers that Mr. Bartholomew had so carefully constructed seemed to waver.

She believed that there was a sliver of goodness buried within him—a glimmer of a lost soul yearning for redemption. It was that belief, however naïve, that kept her entangled in the dangerous dance they shared.

Their interactions became a delicate balance between passion and peril, trust and suspicion. Evelina found herself caught between two worlds—the newfound freedom she had fought for and the allure of a man who embodied both danger and seduction.

As their relationship continued to deepen, Evelina became acutely aware of the risks involved. She understood that her actions had the potential to unravel all the progress they had made, to plunge the mansion back into the depths of darkness from which they had fought so hard to emerge.

Yet, she couldn't deny the intensity of their connection—the way his touch ignited a fire within her, the way his words seemed to unravel the layers of her soul. It was a dance of power and surrender, of attraction and repulsion, that defied logic and reason.

But Evelina knew that she couldn't continue on this treacherous path indefinitely. She grappled with the choice between self-preservation and the desire to save Mr. Bartholomew from the demons that plagued him.

The mansion stood as a constant reminder of the battles fought and the wounds inflicted. It whispered cautionary tales of the consequences that awaited those who danced too close to the flames of desire and deception.

In the depths of her soul, Evelina yearned for a love that transcended the shadows—a love that was built on trust, respect, and a shared commitment to healing. She questioned whether such a love could ever exist with a man so deeply entrenched in his own darkness.

And so, Evelina stood at a crossroads, her heart and mind in a constant struggle. The path she chose would shape not only her own destiny but also the fate of the mansion and its inhabitants.

The dangerous attraction between Evelina and Mr. Bartholomew lingered, its pull unyielding. The question remained: would they succumb to the flames of their desires, risking everything they had fought for, or would they find the strength to break free from the shadows that threatened to consume them both?

Section 4: Survival and Redemption

Subchapter 10: Fighting Back

Evelina had reached her breaking point. The allure of Mr. Bartholomew's charisma and the dangerous attraction that had ensnared her heart were no longer enough to keep her captive in the web of shadows. She had seen the destructive power of his manipulation, and she was determined to fight back.

Gathering her strength and resolve, Evelina began to devise a plan—a plan to protect herself and those who remained vulnerable to Mr. Bartholomew's control. She sought allies among the staff and other individuals who had felt the weight of his manipulation, forming a united front against the patriarch's reign.

Together, they developed strategies to expose his tactics and undermine his influence. They dug deeper into the family's secrets, unearthing evidence that would shed light on Mr. Bartholomew's true nature. Evelina was determined to expose him for the manipulator he was, no matter the cost.

As word spread of their resistance, fear began to take hold within the mansion. Mr. Bartholomew's grip on power weakened as those who had once cowered in his presence found solace in the strength of their unity. They refused to be victims any longer.

Evelina emerged as a beacon of hope—a symbol of resilience and redemption. She used her newfound voice to inspire others, urging them to find the courage to stand up against their oppressor. Her determination and unwavering spirit ignited a fire within the hearts of those who had long suffered under Mr. Bartholomew's control.

But the fight was not without its challenges. Mr. Bartholomew, sensing the threat to his power, fought back with every weapon at his disposal. He unleashed a torrent of manipulation, employing tactics designed to undermine their unity and crush their rebellion.

Evelina found herself facing psychological warfare, as Mr. Bartholomew attempted to exploit her vulnerabilities and manipulate her emotions. It was a dangerous game of cat and mouse—a battle of wills and a fight for survival.

She leaned on her allies, drawing strength from their collective determination. Together, they devised counterstrategies, building a fortress of resilience that could withstand even the most insidious of attacks. They shared their stories, bolstering each other's resolve and reminding themselves of the importance of their fight.

As the battle waged on, Evelina learned the power of her own voice. She stood up to Mr. Bartholomew, confronting him with unwavering strength and unwavering eyes. She refused to be swayed by his manipulations, seeing through his facade to the emptiness that lay beneath.

Her actions sent shockwaves through the mansion, challenging the very foundations of Mr. Bartholomew's power. The residents, once held captive by fear, began to find their own voices, adding their stories to the growing chorus of resistance.

In the face of their united front, Mr. Bartholomew's control began to crumble. The web of shadows that had haunted the mansion for far too long unraveled with each revelation, exposing the true extent of his manipulations.

Evelina's fight for survival became a fight for redemption—for herself, for the mansion, and for the souls that had been trapped within its walls. The battle was far from over, but with each victory, they inched closer to reclaiming their freedom.

As the light of truth pierced through the darkness, Evelina saw glimpses of the future—a future where the mansion would no longer be a place of fear and manipulation. It would become a sanctuary, a symbol of resilience and the triumph of the human spirit.

And in the depths of her soul, Evelina held onto the hope that, through their collective strength and determination, they would emerge from the shadows stronger than ever before—a testament to the power of survival and the resilience of the human heart.

Subchapter 11: Unmasking the Villain

Evelina's relentless pursuit of the truth had led her down a treacherous path, but she had finally uncovered the true identity and intentions of the patriarch. The shocking revelation sent shivers down her spine, as she realized the extent of the danger that had loomed over the mansion.

It was a stormy night when Evelina gathered the residents of the mansion in the grand hall, their faces etched with a mixture of curiosity and apprehension. She took a deep breath, her voice steady but laced with an underlying tremor, as she began to reveal the truth that had been hidden in the shadows for far too long.

"I have discovered the true identity of our patriarch," Evelina announced, her words echoing through the hall. "His name is not Bartholomew, but rather... Theodore Montague."

Gasps filled the room as the revelation hung heavy in the air. The man they had trusted, the man who had held them captive in his web of shadows, had been masquerading under a false name.

Evelina continued, her voice gaining strength. "Theodore Montague is not the benevolent figure he portrayed himself to be. He came to this mansion with a sinister purpose—to exploit our vulnerabilities, to control our lives, and to manipulate us for his own twisted desires."

The residents exchanged glances, the weight of realization settling upon them. The atmosphere was thick with a mixture of anger, betrayal, and fear. They had been mere pawns in Theodore Montague's grand scheme, unwitting participants in his game of power and control.

But the shocking revelations did not end there. Evelina delved deeper into her discoveries, unmasking Theodore's true intentions. She revealed his plot to acquire the family's wealth and destroy anyone who stood in his way, including those who had once been close to him.

As the truth unraveled, panic spread throughout the mansion. The residents grappled with the realization that their lives had been manipulated by a man whose true nature was far more sinister than they could have ever imagined.

But Theodore Montague was not one to be exposed without a fight. As the dust settled from Evelina's revelation, he emerged from the shadows, his face a mask of cold fury. The once-charismatic patriarch revealed his true colors, his true nature as a manipulative and ruthless villain.

"I warned you, Evelina," he spat, his voice dripping with venom. "You should have stayed in the shadows, content to be a pawn in my game. But now, you have sealed your fate and the fate of all those who dared to defy me."

Theodore's words sent a chill through the room, as the residents braced themselves for the storm that was about to descend upon them. His true intentions exposed, he would stop at nothing to protect his secrets and maintain his grip on power.

Evelina, however, refused to be intimidated. She stood tall, her eyes blazing with determination. "We will not be silenced any longer," she declared, her voice ringing with conviction. "We have seen the true face of the villain who has haunted these halls, and together, we will fight for our freedom."

The battle lines were drawn. The mansion became a battleground, with residents mustering their courage and strength to confront Theodore Montague and the forces he had aligned against them. It was a fight for survival, for justice, and for the restoration of the mansion's true purpose—to be a home of love and light, rather than a breeding ground for darkness and manipulation.

Evelina and her allies rallied the residents, inspiring them to find the strength within themselves to stand up against the villain who had held them captive for far too long. They strategized, devised plans, and prepared for the inevitable clash between good and evil.

As the final confrontation loomed, tension crackled in the air. The mansion became a labyrinth of hidden traps, as Theodore Montague played his final cards in a desperate bid to maintain control. Lives hung in the balance, and Evelina knew that the outcome of this battle would determine the fate of all who resided within those walls.

In the heart of the storm, amidst the chaos and uncertainty, Evelina stood resolute. She had unraveled the web of shadows, exposed the true villain, and united the residents in a fight for their lives. The moment of reckoning had arrived, and the battle for redemption and survival would leave no soul untouched.

The web of shadows that had once suffocated the mansion now stood at the precipice of destruction. The truth had been unveiled, and the residents stood united, ready to face the consequences of their defiance.

In the depths of the mansion, where darkness had reigned for far too long, a flicker of hope emerged. It was the hope of redemption, of breaking free from the clutches of a manipulative puppeteer, and reclaiming their lives and their future.

The battle against Theodore Montague would be one for the ages, a clash that would test the limits of their strength and resilience. But Evelina and her allies were prepared to face the darkness head-on, knowing that their fight was not only for themselves but for all those who had suffered under the weight of manipulation.

The final showdown awaited, and Evelina stood at the forefront, ready to lead her comrades into battle. With every step, she carried the hopes and dreams of those who had long been silenced. In the face of adversity, she would prove that the power of truth and unity could conquer even the darkest of shadows.

And as the mansion trembled with anticipation, Evelina whispered a silent prayer, her voice filled with determination and resolve. "We will overcome," she vowed. "We will emerge from this battle stronger, united, and free from the chains that once bound us. The web of shadows will crumble, and light will shine once more."

Subchapter 12: The Final Showdown

The moment of reckoning had arrived. Evelina stood at the heart of the mansion, facing the patriarch, Theodore Montague, in a confrontation that would decide the fate of everyone involved. The air crackled with tension as their gazes locked, each filled with determination and an unyielding resolve.

"You will not win, Theodore," Evelina declared, her voice steady despite the adrenaline coursing through her veins. "Your reign of power ends here."

Theodore's lips curled into a sinister smile, a mixture of arrogance and malice. "Oh, my dear Evelina," he sneered. "You underestimate the lengths I will go to protect what is rightfully mine. I have built this empire, and I will not let you or anyone else tear it down."

Evelina felt a surge of anger fueling her resolve. She had seen the truth, unmasked the villain, and united the residents against Theodore's reign of manipulation. She knew she had to face him head-on, risking everything for the chance to restore justice and freedom to those who had suffered under his control.

The battle erupted in a whirlwind of chaos. Theodore's henchmen emerged from the shadows, loyal to their master and ready to do his bidding. Evelina's allies, armed with determination and a fierce desire for liberation, stood by her side, prepared to face any obstacle that stood in their way.

The clash of wills and power echoed through the mansion. Punches were thrown, words were exchanged like daggers, and lives hung in the balance. The walls of the mansion trembled under the weight of the struggle, as if mirroring the internal turmoil that had consumed its inhabitants for far too long.

Evelina fought with a ferocity she never knew she possessed. Her movements were swift and calculated, fueled by her determination to protect those she cared for and to bring an end to Theodore's reign of terror. She evaded blows, countered attacks, and unleashed her own strikes, each one propelled by the collective strength and resilience of those who had suffered under Theodore's manipulation.

As the battle raged on, Evelina's allies fought alongside her, their spirits unyielding. Together, they formed an unbreakable bond, a force that stood against the darkness and refused to be silenced. Their unity and unwavering determination were a testament to the power of hope and the resilience of the human spirit.

Amidst the chaos, Evelina's gaze locked with Theodore's once more. She saw a flicker of fear in his eyes, a realization that his hold on power was slipping through his fingers. He fought desperately, using every trick in his arsenal to regain control, but Evelina remained steadfast, unyielding in her pursuit of justice.

The battle reached its climax in a clash of titanic proportions. Evelina and Theodore faced each other one final time, their eyes filled with fire and determination. In a moment that seemed to stretch for eternity, Evelina delivered a decisive blow, toppling Theodore to the ground.

As Theodore lay defeated, Evelina approached him, her voice laced with a mixture of triumph and compassion. "Your reign of manipulation ends here, Theodore," she declared. "You can no longer control us. We are free."

With those words, the web of shadows that had ensnared the mansion for so long began to unravel. The residents emerged from the darkness, their faces etched with relief and a renewed sense of purpose. They had triumphed over their captor, and now they would rebuild their lives, free from the suffocating grip of manipulation.

Evelina's bravery and unwavering resolve had shattered the chains that once bound them. She had risked everything, confronted the villain, and emerged victorious. The mansion, once a symbol of darkness and deception, would now become a testament to resilience and redemption.

As the dust settled, Evelina turned to her companions, her voice filled with gratitude and hope. "We have faced the darkness together and emerged stronger," she said. "Let us rebuild this mansion, not as a monument to pain and betrayal, but as a sanctuary of healing and unity."

And so, the residents of the mansion embarked on a journey of healing and transformation. They supported one another, mending the wounds inflicted by Theodore's manipulation and forging a new path toward a brighter future.

The web of shadows had been unraveled, and in its place, a tapestry of resilience, redemption, and newfound strength was woven. The mansion, once haunted by secrets and deception, became a symbol of triumph and the indomitable human spirit.

As the residents moved forward, their hearts filled with hope, Evelina stood tall, knowing that she had played a pivotal role in their liberation. The journey had been arduous, but it had also revealed the depths of courage and resilience within her.

With a renewed sense of purpose, Evelina set her sights on a future free from the shackles of the past. She would carry the lessons learned from the web of shadows, forever mindful of the power of truth, unity, and the unyielding strength of the human spirit.

And as the sun cast its warm rays upon the mansion, illuminating the path ahead, Evelina took a deep breath, ready to embrace the possibilities of a life unburdened by the darkness of the past. The journey had been long, but the rewards were immeasurable.

The web of shadows had been shattered, and in its wake, a new chapter had begun.

Section 5: Resolution and Redemption

Subchapter 13: Redemption and Forgiveness

In the aftermath of the battle, as the mansion stood as a symbol of triumph and resilience, Evelina found herself facing the weight of her choices. She had risked everything to confront the patriarch and bring an end to the web of shadows that had ensnared them all. Now, she had to navigate the path of redemption and find a way to rebuild her own life.

The scars of the past still lingered, and Evelina carried the burden of her actions. She had made sacrifices, challenged her own boundaries, and stepped into the role of a warrior. But with victory came introspection, and she questioned the toll that her journey had taken on her soul.

As she walked through the mansion's halls, she saw the faces of those she had fought alongside, each one bearing their own wounds, physical and emotional. They had all played a part in the unraveling of the web of shadows, and now they sought solace and healing.

Evelina realized that forgiveness was the key to moving forward. Not only forgiving others, but also forgiving herself for the choices she had made in the pursuit of justice. She knew that redemption lay not in erasing the past, but in learning from it and embracing a future defined by compassion and growth.

She approached each person affected by the patriarch's manipulation, offering words of understanding and empathy. She listened to their stories, shared their pain, and reassured them that the web of shadows would no longer define their lives. Together, they embarked on a journey of healing, united by their shared experiences and the newfound strength that came from overcoming adversity.

Evelina's own journey of redemption was intertwined with the journey of those she had fought alongside. They supported one another, offering forgiveness and understanding as they rebuilt their lives, piece by piece. The mansion, once a prison of secrets, became a sanctuary of healing, filled with the warmth of shared laughter and renewed hope.

In her solitude, Evelina reflected on the power of forgiveness. She understood that it was not a single act, but a continuous practice. It required vulnerability and a willingness to let go of resentment, embracing the freedom that forgiveness brought. It was a process, a journey in itself.

She sought solace in the quiet corners of the mansion, surrounded by the echoes of the past. Through introspection and self-reflection, she found the strength to forgive herself. She acknowledged her flaws, her mistakes, and the choices she had made out of necessity. With each step forward, she released the weight of guilt and allowed herself to embrace the possibility of redemption.

As the mansion flourished with life once more, Evelina realized that the journey of redemption was not just about forgiving and healing oneself, but also about extending forgiveness to others. She saw the transformative power of compassion and understanding, how it mended broken relationships and brought solace to wounded hearts.

In the process of rebuilding their lives, the residents of the mansion discovered the power of collective forgiveness. They let go of the past, embracing a future where the web of shadows no longer held sway over their lives. It was a testament to the resilience of the human spirit and the capacity for growth and change.

Evelina stood before her reflection in the mirror, her eyes filled with a newfound sense of clarity and purpose. She had journeyed through darkness, faced her own demons, and emerged on the other side with a heart open to forgiveness and a spirit yearning for redemption.

The road ahead was still uncertain, but Evelina knew that as long as she held forgiveness in her heart, she would find the strength to face whatever challenges lay in her path. With renewed determination, she stepped into the future, ready to embrace the possibilities of a life shaped not by the shadows of the past, but by the light of redemption and forgiveness.

Subchapter 14: Unraveling the Web

As the mansion basked in the healing light of redemption, Evelina and the other characters continued their quest for truth. The web of shadows had ensnared them for far too long, and now they were determined to unravel its intricate threads and find closure.

Together, they embarked on a relentless pursuit of the truth, digging deeper into the past and unearthing long-buried secrets. With each revelation, the pieces of the puzzle fell into place, revealing a web of interconnected betrayals, hidden agendas, and long-held grudges.

Evelina's determination never wavered as she followed the twisted path that led to the heart of the web. She faced dangerous adversaries and walked through the corridors of her own fears, refusing to let the darkness consume her. Alongside her allies, she confronted the ghosts of the past, seeking answers that would finally bring closure to the mansion's troubled history.

As the layers of deception were peeled away, the truth emerged like a beacon of light in the darkness. It was a truth that had the power to shatter illusions, to mend broken relationships, and to offer solace to wounded souls.

In the midst of their investigation, Evelina and her companions discovered that the patriarch, Theodore, had not acted alone in orchestrating the web of shadows. Behind him stood a shadowy network of individuals, each driven by their own motivations and desires for power.

The unraveling of the web brought with it a sense of relief and understanding. The characters found solace in knowing that they had not been mere pawns in a game of manipulation, but rather victims of a complex scheme. The revelation of the truth allowed them to reclaim their agency, to see themselves as survivors rather than victims.

With the truth exposed, the characters faced a crossroads. Some sought vengeance, their hearts consumed by anger and a thirst for justice. Others, like Evelina, understood that closure and healing came not through vengeance, but through forgiveness and letting go of the past.

In the aftermath of the revelation, the characters found themselves grappling with their own emotions and inner demons. They confronted the choices they had made, the mistakes they had committed, and the pain they had endured. Through heartfelt conversations and moments of vulnerability, they began the journey of self-forgiveness and reconciliation.

Evelina, in particular, emerged as a beacon of strength and compassion. She extended her hand to those who had hurt her, offering forgiveness and understanding. She recognized that holding onto anger and resentment would only perpetuate the web of shadows in her own heart. Instead, she chose to break free from its grasp, embracing the power of forgiveness as a path to personal healing.

As the characters found closure, they also discovered newfound connections and bonds. They supported one another, providing comfort and reassurance as they navigated the complexities of their shared past. The mansion, once a place of darkness, became a sanctuary of healing and growth.

In the wake of the revelations, the characters made a collective decision to honor the past while embracing the future. They transformed the mansion into a place of refuge, opening its doors to others who had suffered under the weight of their own webs of shadows.

The final chapter of their journey was marked by the triumph of resilience and the power of forgiveness. Evelina, now a symbol of strength and redemption, looked out over the mansion's grounds, her heart filled with a profound sense of peace. The web of shadows that had once ensnared them all had been unraveled, and in its place stood a community bonded by shared experiences and the courage to face their own demons.

As the sun set on the mansion, casting long shadows across the landscape, Evelina whispered a heartfelt farewell to the past. The journey had been arduous, filled with pain and uncertainty, but it had also been a testament to the indomitable human spirit and the capacity for growth and change.

With a renewed sense of purpose and a spirit unburdened by the weight of the web of shadows, Evelina and her companions stepped forward into the future, ready to embrace the limitless possibilities that awaited them. Their journey had come full circle, and they were finally free to live their lives on their own terms, guided by the lessons learned from unraveling the web.

Subchapter 15: A New Dawn

As the first rays of sunlight painted the sky with hues of gold and pink, Evelina stood at the threshold of the mansion, ready to leave the shadows behind and embrace a new beginning. The journey she had embarked upon had changed her in ways she could never have imagined. She had faced darkness, battled her inner demons, and emerged stronger than ever before.

With a sense of liberation in her heart, Evelina stepped out into the world beyond the mansion's gates. The cool morning breeze brushed against her face, carrying with it a promise of endless possibilities. She carried the lessons learned and the strength gained throughout her tumultuous journey, ready to face whatever lay ahead.

Her time within the mansion had taught her the value of self-discovery and the importance of staying true to oneself. Evelina had come to understand that she was not defined by her past or the shadows that had threatened to engulf her. She had found her voice, her resilience, and her unwavering determination to create a life of her own choosing.

Leaving the mansion behind was bittersweet. It had been a place of darkness and secrets, but it had also been the crucible where Evelina's spirit had been forged. She had formed deep bonds with the companions who had shared her journey, and while they were parting ways, their connection would forever remain in her heart.

As Evelina ventured into the unknown, she found solace in the beauty of the natural world that surrounded her. The vibrant colors of the blooming flowers and the melodies of birdsong whispered to her soul, reminding her of the simple joys that awaited her outside the confines of the mansion.

With each step, she embraced the freedom to shape her own destiny. Evelina's path led her to new places, new faces, and new opportunities. She embraced the unfamiliar with an open heart, knowing that the experiences she had endured had prepared her for whatever challenges lay ahead.

Along her journey, she encountered individuals whose lives intersected with her own, each one carrying their own burdens and seeking their own forms of redemption. Evelina's newfound strength and empathy allowed her to extend a helping hand, to offer support and understanding to those she met along the way.

She discovered that her story, intertwined with the stories of others, formed a tapestry of resilience and hope. As she listened to their tales of triumph and tribulation, she realized that she was not alone in her struggles. Together, they forged a community of survivors, bonded by their shared experiences and their unwavering determination to live authentically and free from the shackles of the past.

Evelina's journey also led her to places of profound introspection. In quiet moments of solitude, she contemplated the meaning of forgiveness and the power of second chances. She recognized that the truest form of redemption lay in extending compassion to oneself and others, in acknowledging the mistakes of the past, and in embracing the opportunity for growth and transformation.

As the days turned into weeks, and the weeks into months, Evelina's spirit blossomed like the flowers she encountered along her path. She discovered hidden talents and pursued new passions, each endeavor a testament to her newfound confidence and self-belief.

In the midst of her personal growth, Evelina never forgot the lessons learned within the mansion's walls. She remained vigilant, recognizing the signs of manipulation and deceit that had once ensnared her. She used her experiences as a guiding compass, ensuring that she never allowed herself to be trapped in the web of shadows again.

With each chapter of her journey, Evelina's resilience grew stronger, her capacity for love and forgiveness expanded, and her spirit radiated with a luminous strength that drew others towards her. She became a beacon of hope, inspiring those she encountered to face their own shadows and find the courage to step into the light.

As she reflected on her journey, Evelina realized that it was not just about her individual transformation. It was about the collective power of resilience and redemption, about the human capacity to overcome adversity and find solace in the beauty of life's simplest moments.

In the end, it was not the destination that mattered, but the path she had taken to get there. Evelina had emerged from the darkness, carrying the light of her experiences with her. With a heart filled with gratitude and a spirit filled with hope, she continued her journey, embracing the new dawn that awaited her.

Section 6: Epilogue

Subchapter 16: Reflections

As Evelina sat in the quiet solitude of her favorite spot in the park, she allowed her mind to wander back to the events that had unfolded within the walls of the mansion. It had been a tumultuous journey, one that had tested her in ways she had never thought possible. Now, as she reflected on those moments, she felt a sense of gratitude for the lessons learned and the person she had become.

The nature of power had been a central theme throughout her journey. In the mansion, she had witnessed firsthand the ways in which power could be wielded as a weapon, used to manipulate and control those who were deemed less powerful. The patriarch, with his charm and charisma, had been the epitome of this abuse of power. But Evelina had come to understand that true power lay not in the ability to control others, but in the strength to rise above such manipulation and create a life of authenticity and integrity.

Betrayal had also left its mark on Evelina's soul. She had trusted those who had turned out to be wolves in sheep's clothing, disguising their true intentions behind masks of kindness. The wounds inflicted by betrayal had been deep, but they had also taught her the importance of discernment and self-preservation. Evelina had learned to listen to her intuition, to recognize the subtle signs of deception, and to protect her heart from those who sought to harm her.

Survival had been her ultimate goal within the mansion's web of shadows. Every day had presented new challenges, and Evelina had fought tooth and nail to reclaim her autonomy and escape the clutches of the patriarch. She had tapped into reserves of strength she hadn't known existed, drawing from her inner well of resilience and determination. In doing so, she had discovered that survival was not just about physical escape, but also about preserving her spirit and reclaiming her sense of self.

As she contemplated these themes, Evelina found herself drawn to the wisdom that had emerged from her experiences. She realized that power, betrayal, and survival were not isolated concepts, but interconnected threads that wove together the tapestry of human existence. In understanding one, she had come to understand the others, and in doing so, she had gained a deeper understanding of the complexities of the human condition.

But amidst the darkness and the pain, Evelina also found solace in the moments of light and beauty that had shone through. She had discovered the strength of human connection, the power of friendship, and the resilience of the human spirit. These were the moments that had sustained her, that had reminded her of the inherent goodness that resided within every individual.

As she sat in the park, surrounded by the serenity of nature, Evelina realized that her journey within the mansion had been a catalyst for profound personal growth. It had shaken her to her core, but it had also unearthed strengths and qualities she hadn't known she possessed. She had learned to navigate the shadows, to confront her fears, and to emerge with a renewed sense of purpose and self-belief.

With each passing day, Evelina vowed to carry the lessons of the mansion with her. She would never forget the power of resilience, the importance of trust, and the necessity of staying true to oneself. She would use her experiences to guide her actions, to build a life filled with authenticity, compassion, and a commitment to creating a world where power was wielded responsibly and betrayal was replaced with trust.

As she gazed at the beauty of the setting sun, Evelina felt a deep sense of gratitude for the journey she had undertaken. It had been a bittersweet path, filled with pain and triumph, but it had ultimately led her to a place of self-discovery and inner peace. She had emerged from the shadows stronger, wiser, and ready to embrace the future with open arms.

With a contented sigh, Evelina stood up from the bench and began to walk towards the horizon, her heart filled with hope and a newfound sense of purpose. The journey within the mansion had come to an end, but the journey of her life continued, and she was ready to face whatever lay ahead, armed with the lessons and resilience she had gained.

Subchapter 17: Moving On

With the weight of the past gradually lifting from her shoulders, Evelina took a deep breath and let it out, feeling a renewed sense of freedom. It was time to move on, to embrace the future that awaited her with open arms.

Leaving behind the mansion and all its haunting memories, Evelina set out on a journey to rebuild her life. She knew that it would not be easy, that there would still be moments when the shadows of the past would try to creep back in. But she was determined to face those moments head-on, armed with the strength and resilience she had cultivated.

As she ventured into the world, Evelina sought out new opportunities and experiences. She enrolled in classes to pursue her passions, eager to learn and grow in areas that had always intrigued her. She surrounded herself with positive influences, seeking out friendships and connections that would uplift and inspire her.

But it wasn't just about external changes. Evelina knew that true transformation began from within. She delved deep into self-reflection, exploring her own desires, dreams, and values. She embraced the importance of self-care, prioritizing her mental and emotional well-being. Through therapy and self-discovery, she confronted the lingering scars of her past, acknowledging them and learning to let go.

As days turned into weeks and weeks into months, Evelina gradually felt the weight of the shadows fading further into the distance. She discovered moments of joy and laughter, small victories that affirmed her journey towards healing and growth. The future no longer seemed daunting; instead, it held the promise of endless possibilities.

One step at a time, Evelina began to build a life that was true to herself. She pursued a career that resonated with her passions, finding fulfillment in work that allowed her to make a positive impact on others. She nurtured meaningful relationships, surrounding herself with individuals who supported and encouraged her to be the best version of herself.

But amidst all the changes, Evelina never forgot the lessons she had learned within the mansion's walls. The memories, although painful, served as reminders of her strength and resilience. She carried them as reminders of the depths she had traversed and the person she had become.

The shadows of the past no longer defined her. They were merely part of her story, guiding her towards a future filled with hope and determination. Evelina realized that her journey within the mansion had been a catalyst for growth, a crucible that had forged her into a stronger and more resilient individual.

With each passing day, Evelina took pride in the person she was becoming. She celebrated her victories, no matter how small, and acknowledged her own worth. The future held endless possibilities, and she was ready to embrace them with an open heart and a determined spirit.

As she gazed into the horizon, Evelina felt a sense of gratitude for the journey she had undertaken. The shadows had tested her, but they had also revealed her inner strength and resilience. She was no longer defined by the pain and betrayal; she was defined by her ability to rise above it, to carve a path towards a brighter future.

And so, with hope in her heart and determination in her steps, Evelina walked forward into the unknown, ready to create a life that was truly her own. The shadows of the past were fading behind her, replaced by the radiant light of her own strength and the promise of a new beginning.

And as she embarked on this new chapter, Evelina knew that she would forever carry the lessons learned within the web of shadows. They were a reminder of her resilience, her capacity to overcome, and her unwavering spirit. The journey within the mansion had transformed her, and now, she was ready to embrace the beauty of the world beyond.

The End.

Subchapter 18: The Legacy of Shadows

As Evelina moved forward in her journey of healing and growth, she couldn't help but reflect on the legacy of the web of shadows that had plagued the mansion. She had emerged from its clutches, but she knew that there were others out there who might still be ensnared in similar darkness.

With a newfound sense of purpose, Evelina made a solemn vow to herself: she would do everything in her power to prevent others from falling victim to the same shadows that had once consumed her. She understood the importance of shedding light on the hidden dangers and manipulations that lurked beneath seemingly ordinary facades.

Evelina began by seeking out opportunities to share her story. She spoke at local community events, support groups, and even started a blog where she shared her experiences and insights. Her words resonated with those who had faced similar trials, offering them hope and the reassurance that they were not alone.

But Evelina's mission extended beyond just raising awareness. She became an advocate for survivors of abuse and manipulation, lending her voice to organizations that worked tirelessly to provide support and resources to those in need. She volunteered her time and expertise, offering a listening ear and guidance to those who were navigating their own journeys to healing.

Through her advocacy work, Evelina discovered a network of survivors, each with their own stories to tell. They became a community of strength and resilience, supporting one another as they fought to reclaim their lives. Together, they worked to dismantle the web of shadows that threatened to ensnare others, shining a light on the patterns of power and manipulation that perpetuated abuse.

Evelina also recognized the importance of education and prevention. She collaborated with schools, community centers, and organizations to develop workshops and programs aimed at empowering individuals with knowledge and awareness. By equipping others with the tools to identify and resist manipulation, she hoped to break the cycle of abuse and protect future generations from falling prey to the shadows.

In her efforts to prevent others from enduring the same pain and betrayal she had experienced, Evelina discovered a sense of fulfillment and purpose. It was as if her own journey had prepared her for this mission, and she was determined to make a difference in the lives of those who were still trapped in the web of shadows.

But even as she fought for justice and healing, Evelina understood that the process would not be without its challenges. There were moments when doubt crept in, when the weight of the past threatened to overwhelm her. Yet, she drew strength from the resilience she had cultivated, reminding herself of the progress she had made and the lives she had touched.

Evelina knew that her work was not in vain. With each person she helped, each survivor she empowered, the legacy of the web of shadows was weakened. Through her efforts, she aimed to create a ripple effect, spreading awareness and breaking down the barriers that allowed manipulation and abuse to persist.

As Evelina continued to advocate and raise her voice, she remained steadfast in her commitment to healing, justice, and prevention. The legacy of the web of shadows would not define her; instead, it would serve as a catalyst for change, a reminder of her own strength and resilience.

And as she dedicated herself to this cause, Evelina found solace and purpose. She knew that she was making a difference, one person at a time, one step at a time. The shadows that had once threatened to consume her were now a source of strength, propelling her forward as she fought for a world where no one would have to endure the pain and betrayal she had faced.

In her quest to prevent others from falling victim to the web of shadows, Evelina realized that she had become a beacon of light for those still trapped in darkness. And as she looked ahead, she was filled with hope—hope that her efforts would contribute to a world where power was wielded responsibly, where manipulation was exposed, and where survivors could find healing and reclaim their lives.

The legacy of the web of shadows would forever be intertwined with Evelina's own story. But through her resilience, her advocacy, and her unwavering determination, she would ensure that its grip on others would be weakened, replaced by a future where strength, empathy, and justice prevailed.

And so, with a resolute heart and a steadfast spirit, Evelina embarked on her mission, ready to leave a lasting impact on the lives of those affected by the web of shadows.

The End.

Printed in Great Britain
by Amazon

32921981R00056